This is 1929 ya know!

— Look, it's the Hindenbob!

EUROPE

Constantinople (not Istanbul!)

me-o my-o me-o, we sail home from Cairo!

PERSIA

ARABIA

Nile up the ...then sail

Belgian

we bob along rather nicely......

Scotty finds Bob (and what a find!) Congo

INDIAN OCEAN

M.

THE WANDERINGS

AND

ADVENTURES OF

DINOSAUR

B O B

AND THE FAMILY

LAZARDO

DINOSAUR BOB

AND HIS ADVENTURES WITH THE FAMILY LAZARDO

by William Joyce

ATHENEUM
Books for Young Readers
New York London Toronto Sydney New Delhi

THE LAZARDOS were an interesting family. Every year, before the start of baseball season, they'd take a trip far from their beloved home in Pimlico Hills.

"Travel is adventure. Adventure makes you homesick, and baseball makes everything A-OK," explained Dr. Lazardo.

The Lazardos always returned from their journeys with some amazing treasure.

"I wonder what they'll drag back this time?" groused jealous Mrs. DeGlumly, the mayor's wife.

The Lazardos zipped about from one spot on the globe to another: London, Rome, Zanzibar, Cleveland.

While they were on safari in Africa, young Scotty Lazardo wandered away from camp and returned with a dinosaur.

"Look what I caught!" he said.

"Can we keep him?" pleaded Scotty's sisters, Zelda and Velma.

"I don't see why not," said Dr. Lazardo.

"He looks kind of like my uncle Bob," said Mrs. Lazardo.

Jumbu, their bodyguard, said nothing.

Scotty patted the dinosaur on the nose. "Bob?" he tried.

The dinosaur smiled and wagged his giant tail.

So they named him Bob.

With Bob along, safari life was fun. They settled into a routine: swimming in the morning, games of baseball in the afternoon, and songs by the campfire before bed.

One night, after a rousing rendition of "The Hokey Pokey," Mrs. Lazardo remarked, "Dancing and dinosaurs, who could ask for anything more?"

One day, while deep in the jungle, they came to the banks of the river Nile. Dr. Lazardo said, "Let's go sailing!"

So they made Bob into a ship and steered him down the river. "Going by Bob is the only way to travel," sighed Zelda. Everyone began to sing "Take Me Out to the Ball Game." Bob hummed along. Jumbu said nothing but tapped his foot. It was grand.

Bob and the Lazardos were becoming quite attached to one another. But they couldn't sail him all the way back to Pimlico Hills.

"Bob took us down the Nile in style," reasoned the doctor. "It would be bad manners if we didn't return the favor."

So Dr. Lazardo booked passage on a luxury liner. Passengers danced the conga up and down Bob's back while he played his trumpet—a gift from the ship's orchestra.

"I think he likes the trumpet," said Scotty.

"I'll write him a song," said Zelda.

Every evening, the children led Bob up to his berth in the ship's smokestacks and brought him a bedtime snack—two peanut-butter-and-bologna sandwiches and four hundred double Dutch chocolate cakes. After a serenade of Zelda's special song, "The Ballad of Dinosaur Bob," Bob always fell asleep with a smile on his face.

Their arrival in New York was quite eventful. Tugboats blew their whistles, freighters blasted their horns, people waved from bridges.

"New York loves a show," said Mrs. Lazardo.

"And Bob's the biggest show in town," said Dr. Lazardo as they gathered up their baggage.

They toured New York, and after a light lunch of 7,500 hot dogs in Central Park, they caught a train to Pimlico Hills. It was Bob's first train ride.

When they arrived in Pimlico Hills, traffic stopped. Dogs barked. People squealed with delight. Mrs. DeGlumly, the mayor's wife, turned pea green with envy.

"That thing's a menace to the community!" she grumped.

"I think he's kinda nice," the mayor said meekly.

The Lazardos began to sing "Pimlico Hills, My Hometown." Bob played his trumpet. The whole town sang along.

Reporters flocked to the Lazardos' house.

"Bob will scare off burglars," Dr. Lazardo told them.

"And he can blow a mean trumpet," said Zelda.

"He Hokey Pokeys like a fool," said Velma.

"And can he play baseball!" shouted Scotty.

Jumbu said nothing.

The photographers' cameras flashed. LENGTHY LIZARD LANDS WITH LAZARDOS read the headline in the paper.

Bob was famous.

Life in Pimlico Hills was restful. There were meals on the lawn, games of Go Fish, and a snack and a serenade before bed each night.

"Home sweet home, eh, Bob?" asked Scotty. Bob smiled and wagged his tail.

One day, Bob and the Lazardos played some baseball in the backyard. Bob could play right and left fields at the same time!

The Pimlico Pirates watched Bob play. The Pirates had never won a game. They were the worst team in history. But everyone in town loved them and went to all their games.

"I wish the big guy in green could play for us," said one of the Pirates.

The following morning, Bob saw some neighborhood dogs chasing cars.

He decided to join them.

"Aren't you the Lazardos' dinosaur?" asked a policeman.

Bob nodded.

He was arrested for disturbing the peace.

Bob enjoyed being fingerprinted. He didn't understand he was in trouble.

The Lazardos rushed to get Bob out of prison. But the mayor wouldn't let him go.

"I'm sorry," he explained. "My wife . . . I mean, we can't have dinosaurs running wild in the streets. We'll be sending him back to Africa in the morning."

Bob let out a sad howl. So did the Lazardos. Everyone—even the policemen—began to cry.

That night, no one at the Lazardos' house could sleep.

"Poor Bob," sighed Scotty.

"All alone," said Velma.

"Without his trumpet," said Zelda.

Suddenly, Dr. Lazardo jumped up, grabbed his hat, and ran out the door.

"Don't worry," said Mrs. Lazardo. "Your father never goes out in his pajamas unless he has a smashing idea."

Soon, the doctor returned with Bob.

"Come on," he whispered. "Be very quiet. We're running away."

Bob's escape made headlines the following morning.

LAZARDOS AND LIZARD ON THE LOOSE. COPS CONFUSED.

So they hit the open road. "If Pimlico Hills won't have Bob, then we won't have Pimlico Hills!" said the doctor.

"It's Bob or bust!" said Mrs. Lazardo.

"Home is where the Bob is!" said Scotty, and they all agreed.

But something just didn't feel right. Zelda wrote a new song: "I'm So Lonesome I Hope I'm Home Sometime Soon."

That night, as they camped out under the stars, no one felt like singing. Scotty read the newspaper. "Baseball season starts tomorrow," he said sadly.

"Well," said Dr. Lazardo, grabbing the family globe. "Time to decide where we're headed."

"Let Bob decide," said Mrs. Lazardo.

Bob thought for a moment, then touched his nose to a point on the globe.

"Pimlico Hills," said Dr. Lazardo. "He touched Pimlico Hills!"

"Home," the children said wistfully.

The next day was the opening game for the Pimlico Pirates. As the stadium filled, no one noticed a large bump in the outfield. Everyone in town was there, including the mayor and his wife, Mrs. DeGlumly.

The team began to run out onto the field. Then the announcer shouted, "And now the newest Pimlico Pirate: **DINOSAUR BOB!**"

The bump began to move. There stood Bob!

The crowd roared. So did the mayor! Mrs. DeGlumly said nothing.

Bob smiled his big dinosaur grin, and the game began.

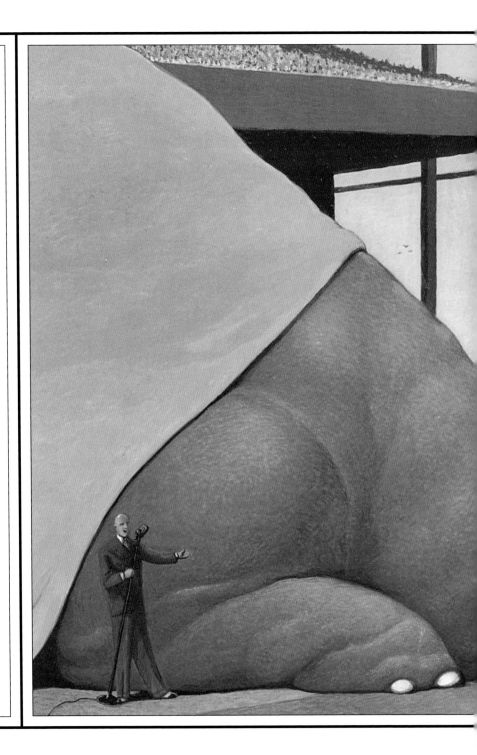

The Lazardos cheered Bob from the dugout and gave him water between innings. The game was close. The Pirates were playing better than they ever had. They needed just one run to win the game when Dinosaur Bob stepped up to bat. He swung with all his might. *CRACK!* The ball went up and up, clear out of the stadium and out of sight!

Bob rounded the bases in three great strides and touched his nose to home plate. For the first time in history, the Pimlico Pirates had won!

The Lazardos rushed onto the field and hugged Bob. The crowd cheered Bob all the way out of the stadium. The mayor cheered the loudest.

Bob was a hero.

"I still say he's a menace to the community," sniffed Mrs. DeGlumly.

"He promises he'll never chase cars again," said Scotty.

The mayor looked at his wife. She frowned. Then he looked at Bob.

Suddenly, Bob kissed Mrs. DeGlumly on the cheek. She was so startled, she stopped frowning.

"He can stay!" said the mayor.

"Hooray!" yelled the Lazardos, and they launched into the Hokey Pokey. The whole town joined in.

That evening, Bob and the Lazardos had a cookout in the backyard. After dinner, Jumbu brought out musical instruments. Scotty on bongos, Bob on trumpet. And everyone else on kazoos.

"Here's to Bob," said Dr. and Mrs. Lazardo.

"The best ball player . . . ," said Velma.

"The best pal . . . ," said Zelda.

"And the best dinosaur a family ever had!" shouted Scotty.

Jumbu smiled.

Zelda began to play "The Ballad of Dinosaur Bob." And they all sang and danced late into the summer night.

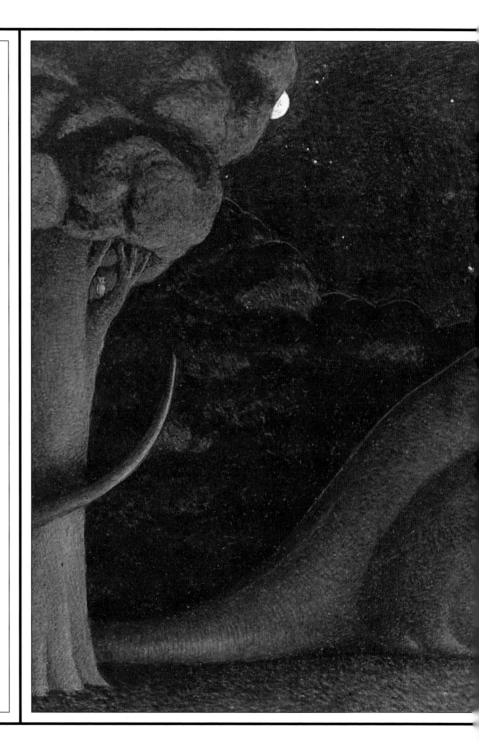

The Ballad of Dinosaur Bob

by Zelda Lazardo

(to the tune of "Auld Lang Syne")

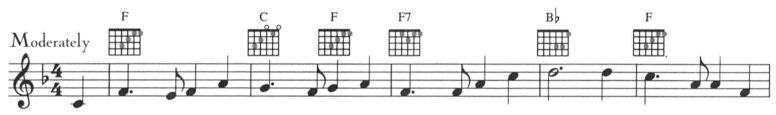

He's Bob, the best old Bob, the big-gest Bob you've ev-er seen. He's Me- so-zo-ic

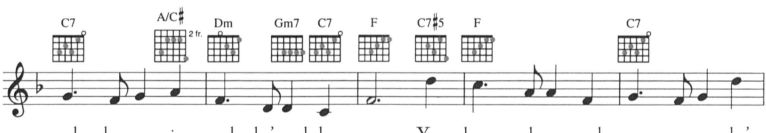

and he-ro-ic, and he's real-ly green. Yes, large and green and so se-rene, he's

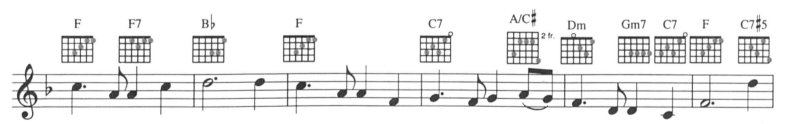

gen-tle and he's sweet, and when the mu-sic plays for him he___ stamps his migh-ty feet. He's

F.   C   F F7 B♭

Bob, the best old Bob, the big-gest Bob you'll ev - er know. He's

F   C7   A/C♯ Dm Gm7 C7 F

Me- so - zo - ic and he - ro - ic, and we love him so.

ATHENEUM BOOKS FOR YOUNG READERS

An imprint of Simon & Schuster Children's Publishing Division

1230 Avenue of the Americas, New York, New York 10020

Copyright © 1988, 1995 by William Joyce

Originally published in 1988 by Laura Geringer Books/HarperCollins Publishers

All rights reserved, including the right of reproduction in whole or in part in any form.

ATHENEUM BOOKS FOR YOUNG READERS is a registered trademark of Simon & Schuster, Inc.

Atheneum logo is a trademark of Simon & Schuster, Inc.

For information about special discounts for bulk purchases, please contact

Simon & Schuster Special Sales at 1-866-506-1949 or business@simonandschuster.com.

The Simon & Schuster Speakers Bureau can bring authors to your live event. For more information or to book an event,

contact the Simon & Schuster Speakers Bureau at 1-866-248-3049 or visit our website at www.simonspeakers.com.

Book design by Alicia Mikles, based on an original design by Christine Kettner.

The text for this book was set in Nicholas Cochin.

The illustrations for this book were rendered in oil and acrylic.

Manufactured in China

0217 SCP

First Atheneum Books for Young Readers Edition

2 4 6 8 10 9 7 5 3 1

CIP data for this book is available from the Library of Congress.

ISBN 978-1-4814-8947-8

ISBN 978-1-4814-8948-5 (eBook)

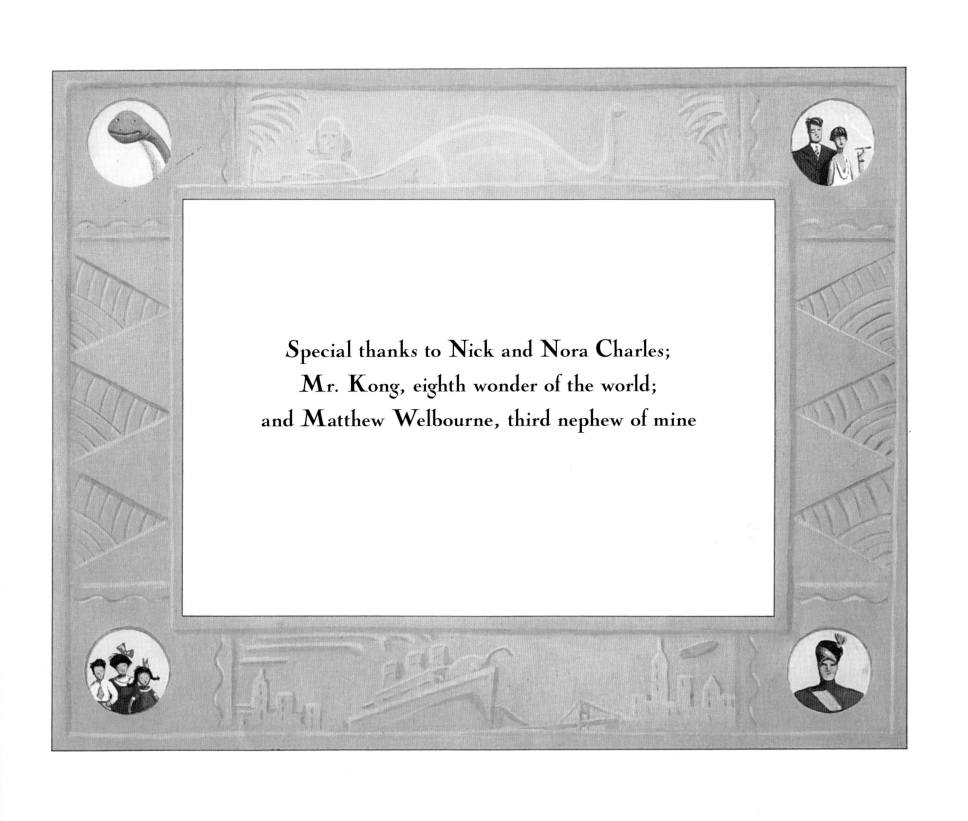

Special thanks to Nick and Nora Charles;
Mr. Kong, eighth wonder of the world;
and Matthew Welbourne, third nephew of mine

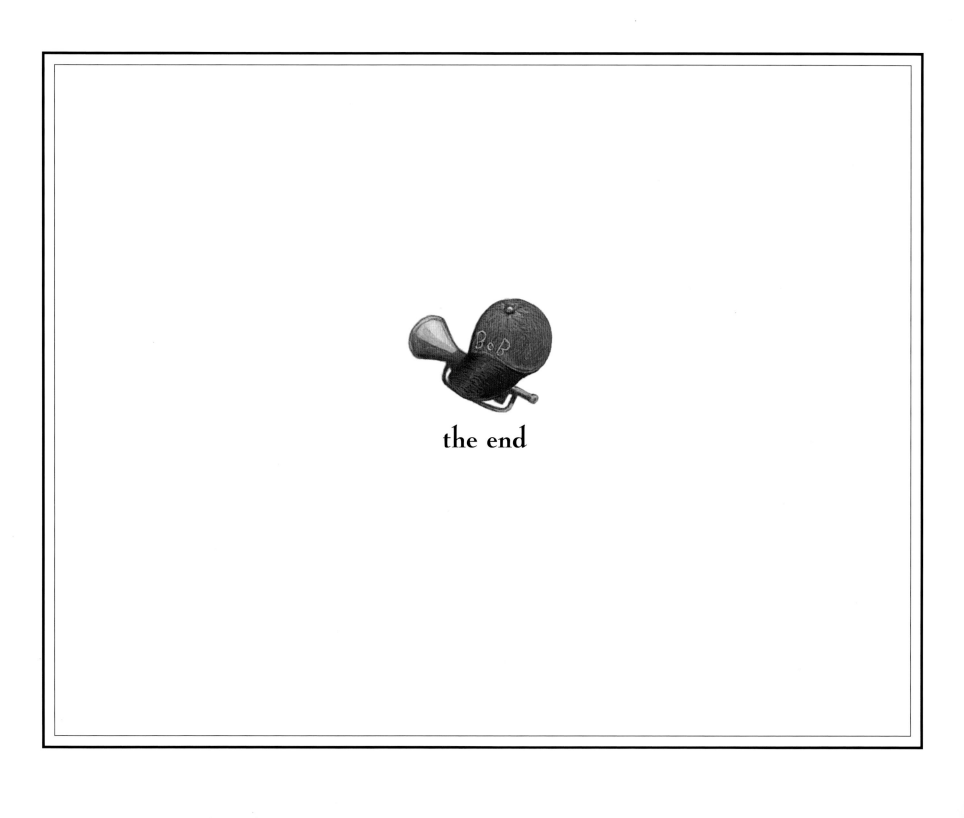

the end